This is Little Wonder, the famous roly-poly pig.
Look at all his prizes.

But once he was just an ordinary piglet.
He was small and shiny and very shy.

Little Wonder

Ian Whybrow

Illustrated by
Emily Bolam

Hodder
Children's
Books

A division of Hodder Headline plc

He was like a sucked pink sweet.
He always had to wait at the
end of the dinner queue.

And his name was – Number 9

He wanted to be very good at something, so he taught himself to roly-poly. His eight brothers and sisters said he was silly.

Then one day he did a very fast roly-poly . . .

through
the door . . .

past the stable . . .

round the tractor . . .

across the meadow . . .

and into the wood.

He was covered in mud and leaves.
Along came a mouse. He said,
"Hello, what are you?"

And the shy little piglet said,
"I am Number 9. I am lost."

The mouse said, "Ah, poor thing.
I think you must be a lost mouse."
The piglet was too shy to say no.
So he had to eat blackberries. Puh!

And the mouse tried to
squeeze him into his house.

Doof!

Along came a noisy rabbit.
He said, "PROBLEMS?"
The mouse said, "This is Number 9.
He is lost and he is not a mouse."
And the noisy rabbit said, "Well, I think
he must be a very mucky rabbit!"

The piglet was too shy to say no.
So he had to eat lettuce. Puh!

And he couldn't do the bunnyhop. whoops!

Along came a squirrel.
She said, "Can I help?"

The noisy rabbit said,
"PROBLEMS!
Our friend, Number 9, is lost.
He's not a mouse.
He's not a mucky rabbit.
What can he be?"

So the squirrel said,
"Let's see if he likes nuts."

The nut went ping like a bar of wet soap.
"Oh dear," said the squirrel.
"He's not a squirrel either."

Down flew a mother birdie.
She said, "Cor, perhaps he is a little birdie,
too young to fly. Help me put him in my nest."

The piglet was too shy
to say no. So the mouse
helped and the noisy rabbit
helped and the squirrel helped.
And up went Number 9,
right up to a nest at the top
of a tall tall tree.

He had to eat worms. Puh!
And the mother birdie sat on
his head.

Doof!

At last, the mother birdie said, "Cor, I don't think you are a birdie after all! What can you be?"

Number 9 was too shy to say. So he did a roly-poly out of the nest, and along the branch. Then he did a roly-poly through the air and . . .

Splash!

He fell into the lake.

The mouse, the noisy rabbit,
the squirrel and the mother birdie rushed to help him.
"What a wonderful roly-poler!" said the mouse.
"What a wonderful diver!" said the noisy rabbit.

"What a wonderful swimmer!" said the squirrel.
"Whatever can this wonderful creature be?"
said the mother birdie.

Out came the piglet, all lovely and shiny like a sucked pink sweet. And all the animals said, "So that's what he is!

He's a piglet!"

The mother birdie flew down.
"Follow me, Little Wonder!" she cawed.
"I'll show you the way home to your sty."

So the piglet followed her, going roly-poly
all the way out of the wood,
across the meadow . . .

round the tractor . . .

past the stable . . .

. . . until, at last, all muddy and mucky,
he rolled through the door of the pigsty.

"Goodbye, Little Wonder!"
called the mother birdie.
"Come and see us again soon."

The proud little pig washed himself under the tap. "I'm not shy and silly and my name is not Number 9!" he said. "I am the famous roly-poler who went to the wood and did a wonderful dive.

And now my name is
Little Wonder!"

"Dinner time!" called Mum.
And all the little piglets raced to get their dinner.
And who do you think was first in the queue?

Yes, it was Little Wonder,
the famous roly-poly pig.

For Jackie and Brian - I. W.

British Library Cataloguing in Publication Data
A catalogue record of this book is available from the British Library

ISBN 0 340 635940 (HB)
ISBN 0 340 635959 (PB)

Text copyright © Ian Whybrow 1999
Illustrations copyright © Emily Bolam 1999

The right of Ian Whybrow to be identified as author
of this work and of Emily Bolam as illustrator of this work
has been asserted by them in accordance
with the Copyright, Design and Patents Act 1988

First published in 1999
by Hodder Children's Books,
a division of Hodder Headline plc,
338 Euston Road, London NW1 3BH

10 9 8 7 6 5 4 3 2 1

Printed in Hong Kong